# Mama Always Comes Home

By Karma Wilson

Illustrated by Brooke Dyer

HARPERCOLLINS*PUBLISHERS*

Manufactured in China.
All rights reserved. No part of this book may be used or reproduced in
any manner whatsoever without written permission except in the
case of brief quotations embodied in critical articles and reviews.
For information address
HarperCollins Children's Books, a division of HarperCollins
Publishers, 1350 Avenue of the Americas, New York, NY 10019.
www.harpercollinschildrens.com

Library of Congress Cataloging-in-Publication Data
Wilson, Karma.    Mama always comes home / by Karma Wilson ;
illustrated by Brooke Dyer.— 1st ed.    p. cm.    Summary: From Mama
Bird to Mama Cat, mothers of all kinds come home to their children.
ISBN-10: 0-06-057505-0 (trade bdg.) — ISBN-13: 978-0-06-057505-2 (trade bdg.)
ISBN-10: 0-06-057506-9 (lib. bdg.) — ISBN-13: 978-0-06-057506-9 (lib. bdg.)
ISBN-10: 0-06-057507-7 (pbk.) — ISBN-13: 978-0-06-057507-6 (pbk.)
[1. Mother and child—Fiction. 2. Animals—Fiction.
3. Stories in rhyme.] I. Dyer, Brooke, ill. II. Title.
PZ8.3.W6976Mam 2005    2003026979    [E]—dc22

Typography by Carla Weise
❖

To beautiful Owen and Zoe
and to their mother, Margaret Anastas,
whose love for her children made this
book a necessity. Thank you, Margaret.
—K.W.

For my mama.
—B.D.

In a softly feathered nest,
a mama bird and hatchlings rest.
Mama always does her best
to keep her babies fed.

But all the little birdies cry
when Mama says she has to fly.
She cuddles each and chirps, "Good-bye,"
then tucks them into bed.

She goes to dig up worms, and then
Mama Bird flies home again.

Mama always comes home.

On a cozy bed of hay,
a barn cat and her kittens lay.
Mama Cat must go away
to have her morning snack.

Her kittens cry to see her go
because they love their mama so.
She kisses all and purrs, "Please know
I'll soon be coming back."

She goes to sip sweet cream, and then Mama Cat strolls home again.

Mama always comes home.

Puppies play out in the sun.
They yip and yelp, they yap and run.
Mama Dog joins in the fun
until she's called away.

She snuggles all before she goes
and licks each puppy on the nose.
She tells them all to try to doze.
But they whine, "Mama, stay!"

She goes to see her boy, and then
Mama Dog runs home again.

Mama always comes home.

Mama Dolphin in the sea,

Mama Chipmunk in the tree,

clever Mama Chimpanzee,

and big old Mama Bear.

Mama Gopher in her hole,

teensy-weensy Mama Mole,

Mama Pony with her foal,

# Mamas everywhere!

They leave their little ones,

but then . . .

They hurry
right back home again.

Mamas always

come home.

In a chair all cozy snug,
a mama gives her child a hug.
She says, "I love you, cuddle bug,
but now I have to go."

Her child cries, "Don't go away!"
And Mama says, "I want to stay,
but while I'm gone have fun and play,
and soon, before you know,
time will fly right by, and then
I'll be coming home again."
Because . . .

Mama always comes back home

to you.